FAITH and the FOREMAN

A HISTORICAL ROMANCE NOVEL

Also by Marsha Ward

FAITH and the FOREMAN

A HISTORICAL ROMANCE NOVELLA

Marsha Ward

WestWard Books

Payson, Arizona

WestWard Books
P O Box 53
Payson, Arizona 85547
www.westwardbooks.com

Publisher's Note: This is a work of fiction. Names, characters, places, and incidents are a product of the author's imagination or are represented fictitiously. Locales and public names are sometimes used for atmospheric purposes. Any resemblance to actual people, living or dead, or to businesses, companies, events, institutions, or locales is completely coincidental.

Cover Design: SelfPubBookCovers.com/FrinaArt
Book Layout © 2017 BookDesignTemplates.com

Faith and the Foreman first appeared in OLD WEST COLLECTION, volume nine of the bestselling and RONE Award-winning Timeless Romance Anthology series.

Faith and the Foreman/ Marsha Ward
ISBN 978-1-947306-20-2
ebook ISBN 978-0-9961463-0-2

Chapter 1

A bell jangled on the horse-drawn street car outside as Faith Bannister folded the letter she'd been reading and rose to pace the room. After two circuits, she stopped before her cousin. "I am ruined."

Clarissa Pembroke looked up from the bandage she was knitting and shook her head. "The news can't be all that bad, dear. We've managed to survive the bank crisis fairly well thus far."

Faith waved the letter. "The interest on my stocks is practically zero."

"You should have told me. I must try harder to find employment." Clarissa breathed heavily. "I can't believe my usefulness as a nurse is over because of a few gray hairs." She straightened her back as though in denial of her age. "I'm going to Doctor Harley's lecture tonight on treating poisons. It could be useful to learn about medical advances."

"You shouldn't have to support me," Faith said. "I'll sell the house to that fat banker, Mr. Spencer. He has wanted it ever since Poppa and

Mama got killed." She bit a fingernail, then, at Clarissa's continuing reproachful look, removed her finger from her teeth. "I know. Mama tried so hard to break me of that." She brushed a curl out of her misty eye and whispered, "Stocks and bonds are no replacement for one's family. I'm most grateful for your companionship."

Clarissa wiped her own tearing eyes.

Faith turned away. "Perhaps I can enter the nursing school at Bellevue Hospital. Mr. Spencer offered a price sufficient for me to pay tuition and rent us an apartment." She shrugged. "I'll have to let the servants go. If it appears I don't have time to train as a nurse before we're destitute, I'll become a governess or a shop clerk."

Clarissa shook herself as though to restore a cheerful outlook. "Let's not fret about finances now, dear. Come with me tonight and enjoy the lecture." She held up her knitting. "This bandage will be finished by then, and I have another eleven for the good doctor."

~*~*~

"Slim! Slim McHenry!"

When Amos Ramsey bellowed his name, Slim changed direction from going toward the bunkhouse to heading for the boss. What did he do to make Mr. Ramsey so angry? He couldn't recall any slip-up today. "Yes, sir?" he said, hoping he still had a job.

"Dan Crowley is leaving. After ten years!" Amos glowered at Slim. "His wife claims he's too busted up to cowboy anymore. She's taking him off to Tucson."

"That's bad news, boss. He's a good foreman."

"You're takin' his place. Ask Dan what to do."

Mr. Ramsey walked off, leaving Slim with his jaw hanging open. *Foreman! He wants me to be foreman?* He whistled in surprise, struck by the man's abrupt manner. Usually Ol' Amos enjoyed conversing with his cowhands, but not tonight. *Could be he's upset about Dan quitting, but he could've been more forthcoming with the details of the job.* He hoped Hoosier Dan was of a mind to enlighten him.

Slim started toward the foreman's little bungalow in back of the main house. If Dan wasn't at supper, Mrs. Crowley would know where he was.

Dan was sitting down to eat, but he took time to shake Slim's hand and give him a rundown on his new responsibilities.

Half an hour later, Slim left, his head swimming and his hand sore from Dan's enthusiastic congratulations. *Each night I check with Ol' Amos about the next day's work, then parcel out the tasks in the morning. I fancy I'm up to the job. Maybe.* Before trepidation took over, he went to eat his own supper, wondering how the cowhands would receive the news.

He supposed he could count on Curly Price to offer congratulations. He and Curly had ridden together for several years and were good friends. Baldy Babbitt would most likely put on a pout, but he wouldn't want the job either. Too much responsibility.

Slim decided none of the other hands would give him more than occasional grief and sass, except Rance Hunter. He snorted. Hunter was a difficult case, prickly as could be. He was the boss's stepson, but there was no love lost between them.

Slim paused to slap the horseshoe hung over the bunkhouse door before he entered to eat. He would need all the luck he could get.

~*~*~

A day later, Faith gasped, tightening her fingers on the day's newspaper. She looked toward Clarissa, her anxiety seeping away.

"I like that bright light in your eye," Clarissa said.

"I have a better plan than nursing school." Faith rose and took the *Times* to Clarissa.

Her cousin looked up from her needles. Three new white bandages lay rolled beside her on the sofa.

"Look." Faith showed her the newspaper page. "Here's an advertisement seeking a school teacher in the West for ten months. The school board will pay transportation costs, provide a living space, groceries, firewood, and they'll pay a salary besides. I can teach mathematics and reading and writing and...even stitchery! Once I sell the house, the proceeds and a teaching post will provide income sufficient for us both."

"Hmm. Teaching will suit you better than nursing." Clarissa resumed her knitting. "How do you win the position?"

Faith crimped the newspaper between her hands. "I must send a telegram immediately to the president of the school board in this town of—" She looked at the advertisement again. "Bitter Springs, Arizona Territory. This will solve our difficulties."

"You must hurry so your answer to the advertisement arrives ahead of any others."

"Yes." Faith hurried to compose a brief message with a list of her academic accomplishments and prepared to go to the telegraph office. "That should serve. Let's pray I'm the most worthy applicant."

"McHenry!"

Slim grunted. *Rance Hunter sounds feisty*

this morning. He turned from saddling his horse to watch Hunter walk toward him. The wiry man at his side had spent the weekend in the bunkhouse with the other hands. The man wore a gun belt that had seen much use, and had pulled his hat low over his eyes.

When the men came near, Slim nodded to them.

"We need another man for the roundup," Hunter said. "This here's Nick Bray. Hire him on."

Surprised at the demand, Slim slipped around the horse to hide his face. He took time to adjust the length of his off stirrup before he looked back toward the men.

He appraised Bray, who inched his hat back with one finger under the brim. The man's inky black eyes gave Slim a moment of pause. What kind of man was this Nick Bray?

Slim finally broke the silence. "Where'd you last work, Bray?"

"New Mexico." He crooked his head toward the east. "A man name of Peterson."

"You handle cattle for him?"

"Steers, mostly. He was shipping."

"What've you done this summer?"

"Rode fence, mostly."

Slim looked at the man for a while longer. Then he asked, "Why'd he let you go?"

"No work." Bray nursed tight black gloves onto his hands.

Slim made a decision. "We can use you for a time. Ride with Hunter. He has no partner right now." He turned to Hunter. "You two take the buckboard and load up the barbed wire from the shed. I sent a crew to fix that break on the Diamond Point fence."

Bray nodded assent. Slim was satisfied, seeing the man was ready to tackle the job.

Apparently Hunter wasn't ready. "My horse needs to be worked," he said.

"Not this morning. We've lost cattle through that break, and your—" Slim stopped short before he said *father*. "Mr. Ramsey wants the job done today."

Hunter's face flamed, but he spun on his heel and stomped over to the wagon yard. Bray kept pace with the angry man. Slim watched for a moment before he bent to pull the cinch tight.

~*~*~

As they approached the equipment shed, Bray glanced at Rance. "You got me hired on. What's the plan?"

Rance slowed his pace. "I want the old skinflint out of the picture. If he gets sick and dies, I'll end up with the whole outfit and be a rich man." He opened the shed door and grabbed a pair of leather gloves. "Put these on. They're thicker than those you got. That blasted wire cuts your hands ragged, and I don't want you bleeding on me."

Bray put the gloves on over his own.

"Pull out about six of them rolls, and I'll go get the buckboard," Rance said.

Bray turned and did as he was told while Rance hitched a team to the buckboard and led the horses to the shed. The men loaded the barbed wire rolls and various tools onto the vehicle, and then Rance grabbed the brake handle and swung himself up onto the seat. He looked down at Bray.

"You coming?"

Bray nodded and climbed into the buckboard. As he sat on the seat he asked, "How do you plan to get rid of your...the old man?"

Rance took the lines. "You know the locoweed plant? I gathered some of them prickly pods and powdered the seeds. That poison will drive a cow mad and kill it. It'll do the same to a man."

"You're going to poison him?"

Rance slapped the lines on the rumps of the team. "Hi! Get up there!" He turned to Bray, grinning. "I already am."

"I think shooting him is better," Bray grunted. "It's quick."

"Nah. All the fingers would point at me. Folks

know we argue. Poison's slow, but it's sure."

Once they arrived at the broken section of fence, they unloaded the barbed wire rolls and tools for the cowhands who were doing the repair. Rance dropped a shovel, then ran to the front of the buckboard, climbed up, grabbed the lines, and started the team. Bray vaulted onto the back of the vehicle to avoid being left behind.

"Hey," he yelled. "What's your hurry?"

Rance muttered over his shoulder, "I don't want them getting the idea I was sent down to mend fence."

Bray climbed over the back of the seat and settled himself. "You could've warned me."

"What's it matter? You made it aboard."

"You're crazy, Hunter," Bray said. Soon they were out of sight of the work crew, and he asked, "How do you get him to take the poison?"

"He drinks a glass of whiskey every night before bed. I put a pinch of powder in the bottle every day or so. He doesn't know why he's getting sick, nor does anyone else."

Bray gave a grudging smile. "So it's working?"

"Oh, yes. You'll see how he acts. Soon I can quit selling off cows." He clucked to the team and slapped them into a run toward the ranch headquarters.

~*~*~

A week after sending the telegram to Bitter Springs, Faith stopped by the telegraph office, as she had been doing the last three days, and found a message addressed to her from Mr. Ralph Perkins, school board president. She hurried to the new apartment to show Clarissa the telegram.

"Cousin, they've hired me. I'm to be a school teacher. He's wiring money for my expenses."

"That's good news, dear."

Faith embraced Clarissa. "Thank you for bearing with me through my financial difficulties. I couldn't have gone on without your kind heart."

A week later, Faith and Clarissa stood on the stoop with a valise and trunk at Faith's feet. Clarissa turned from gazing down the street and took both of Faith's hands in hers. "The cab is coming, dear. I'll worry for you, crossing the country all alone."

Faith squeezed her hands. "You needn't do so, cousin. I'm sure I'll find my way on the trains. Think of it as a great adventure, a breakthrough for womankind." She extracted her hands and retied the ribbons holding down her hat as the cab drew up before them.

"You will be careful?" Clarissa asked. "Don't let strangers near your luggage. And don't talk to anyone suspicious."

"I have my pistol," Faith said, patting the pocket of her duster. "I'll take care; really, I shall." Holding back tears, she patted Clarissa on the shoulder and turned to the waiting cab.

The driver had already placed her trunk and valise in the rear storage area. He handed her up to the seat then took his position and started the horse off with a click of his tongue and a flip of the lines. Faith looked through the back window at Clarissa, who got smaller and smaller in the distance.

At last Faith turned forward on the seat, biting her nail. Would anyone be at her destination to meet her? She'd wired Mr. Perkins the expected date of her arrival, but what if she arrived late? Or early?

I do hope I am not making a mistake.

Chapter 2

Faith took the train conductor's hand, stepped down from the passenger car, and stood at last on the platform of the rustic railroad depot in Winslow, Arizona Territory.

Gripping her valise in one hand and a newspaper she'd purchased at the last stop in the other, she looked around, inhaling deeply to calm her nerves. She immediately choked on unfamiliar scents and the residual smoke from the steam engine. She coughed several times, embarrassed to make such an entrance. If her employer could see her now, he might change his mind at the sight. She straightened her shoulders. Being again on terra firma was a welcome change after the constant motion of the railway cars.

Faith moved away from the train. She turned and saw—with great relief—her trunk being manhandled down the gangplank from the baggage car. She could put to rest her worry that it would remain on the train and travel to San Francisco without her. Now she directed her concern to finding whoever had been sent to meet her, restraining a wild impulse to clutch her duster close about her body and flee back into the familiar train car.

Calm yourself, Faith. You have been well schooled. You are capable of teaching children, though that was never Father's intent in educating you.

She took a breath, a shallow one this time, and looked around. Several people stood on the platform but gradually departed as they met their relatives and friends. Soon the area was cleared of all except a large-boned man whose slouch hat was shoved to the back of his head. He stood a ways off, looking in her direction.

That must be the person sent to meet me, she thought and took a step toward him. The big man must have arrived at the same conclusion, as he began walking toward her.

"'Lo," he called, snatching the hat off his head. "Are you Miss Bannister? Miss Faith Bannister?"

"I am she," Faith replied. *What a large man! Are all Westerners of his size?*

"I'm Clint Dobbs. Mr. Perkins sent me to take you down to Bitter Springs. Let's go." He clapped his hat on his head and turned toward the end of the platform.

"Excuse me," Faith called to his back. "I have a trunk. It's sitting over there." As he turned around, she gestured toward her luggage.

"Oh. Well, I guess you want me to get that." He walked over, easily picked it up, and slung it across his shoulders, then marched off. Faith followed.

Mr. Dobbs led the way to a two-seater buggy, where he shrugged the trunk into the rear seat beside other items covered by a piece of canvas. He took Faith's valise and put it next to the trunk. Then he turned to Faith and picked her up by the waist. The movement surprised her; she gasped as she left the ground. He didn't seem to notice, and set her on the front seat. He went around the buggy, got onto the seat, clucked to the horse, and they were underway at a slow trot, passing through the town in under five minutes.

The next day, after spending the night in the public room of a stage station, Mr. Dobbs brought them into Bitter Springs a half hour after noon. They stopped before a building that Faith figured had to contain a store. Barrels, stacked galvanized buckets, and baskets of produce competed for space under an overhang covering a board walkway.

Mr. Dobbs came around the buggy, lifted Faith down in his accustomed manner, and nodded toward the building. "Mr. Perkins keeps store here, miss. He's the head of the school board."

"Mr. Perkins. Yes, the gentleman with whom I corresponded."

"He'll be pleased to see you're here safe."

"Thank you, Mr. Dobbs. You've been a kind companion."

"Let's get you inside, miss."

Townspeople began to gather around the building, surely wanting to get a glimpse of the new school teacher. Some cast suspicious eyes in Faith's direction. She shuddered but nodded and smiled to those who wished her well and followed Mr. Dobbs into the store, her stomach roiling.

The dark interior blinded her for a moment, but her eyes soon adjusted to the dimness. Before her stood a slight, balding man wearing an enveloping apron, and a woman whose hands fluttered about her face as though she would burst with nervous excitement.

The man took her hand and wrung it. "Here you are at last. I'm Ralph Perkins." He put out his hand to indicate the fidgeting woman. "Faith Bannister, I want to introduce my wife, Edith."

Mrs. Perkins gave a slight curtsey, bobbing her head. "I'm pleased to meet you, Miss Faith. My Curtis and Joey are excited to begin school."

"You'll start teaching next Monday," Mr. Perkins said. "Now that you've arrived, the ladies of our fair town will arrange a dance social at the schoolhouse so everyone can make your acquaintance. Edith, will the dance be a week from Saturday night?"

"Yes. I look forward to it," Mrs. Perkins said.

"How lovely," Faith murmured. *Oh my land!* she thought.

Her driver grinned and said, "The town boys are near crazed waiting to see you. Between them and the cowboys, all your dances will be taken."

Faith smiled back. "I'm sure the social will be a great success." Her throat felt dry as parchment.

"That is our hope, miss," Mr. Dobbs said then turned to Mr. Perkins. "Is your rig out back?" When the storekeeper nodded, Mr. Dobbs said to Faith, "I'll put your things into his buggy and be off to my work."

"Thank you for a pleasant journey, Mr. Dobbs."

As the big man grinned, nodded, and left the store, Mr. Perkins dithered around, seeming to look for something. Finally, he asked, "Where's my hat, Edith? I need to drive Miss Bannister over to the schoolhouse."

Mrs. Perkins fetched the article. "I'll be over to call on you later this afternoon, Miss Faith. I'll bring a box of groceries to start you out."

"You've very kind. Thank you."

Faith climbed into the buggy for the final leg

of her journey. Mr. Perkins got in the driver's seat and turned the horse onto the street.

"We built a little house behind the school, Miss Bannister. You'll set up housekeeping there. The townspeople will bring you wood and groceries. That's part of the fee they pay you for schoolin' their youngsters."

A short time later, Mr. Perkins put Faith's luggage in the little house, said goodbye, and left her.

Faith stood still, eyes closed, taking shallow breaths until she felt her nerves settling. *You will do fine*, she told herself. *You have come this far, and you will not fail.* She slowly opened her eyes, looked around, and set about exploring her world.

Two tiny rooms made up the house, one a kitchen and sitting room, and the other the bedroom. She supposed she was to use the school's privy for sanitary purposes. A pair of shelves hung in the living area, ready for her books. Pans and dishes filled one cupboard, while a second held food staples. The bedroom was just large enough to hold a bed and wardrobe. Faith relaxed her shoulders and began to unpack her trunk.

~*~*~

Slim had kept the hands as busy as he could,

hoping to stay ahead of bad weather, when a storm blustered up, full of thunder and lightning, and everyone had to stay indoors, mending tack and doing similar chores, until it blew over.

While Slim patched a harness, he worried about the boss. Due to blurred vision and dizziness, Mr. Ramsey couldn't ride a horse now. Worse, his manner had changed. For instance, he'd been pretty abrupt that day he'd made Slim the foreman.

When the storm quit, Slim and the hands went outdoors to find that a big lightning-blasted cottonwood tree had fallen and smashed a section of corral fence. Slim assigned a few hands to cut up the tree and mend the fence, but Mr. Ramsey showed up, ranting and raving that they had to leave the tree alone.

"Boss, we got to fix that fence, or the horses will break out and be down the country in no time," Slim said.

"No! Leave it be." Mr. Ramsey raised his arm in a jerky movement, and Slim feared his boss was set to strike him.

"All right," he said. "You're the boss. We'll deal with it another way."

"You see that angel settin' on the tree?"

Slim looked, but there wasn't any holy vision anywhere. "I guess the light's in my eyes, boss," he said.

"You just leave the angel alone, you hear?"

"I hear." Slim swore silently and had the crew pile brush against the break in the fence. Every day, he asked Mr. Ramsey if they could tackle the cottonwood, but every morning, the boss saw something new sitting on the tree. Slim had to go about his work, worrying even more about Ol' Amos.

~*~*~

"I am Miss Bannister," Faith announced to the gathering of pupils early Monday morning. "Let's get acquainted. We'll go one by one around the room. Tell me your names and ages."

Eleven heads nodded. The smallest pupil needed a poke or two from an older girl seated behind her, but she finally began and said that her name was Lovinia Evans. Then she ducked her head, hid her face, and refused to say anything else, despite repeated pokes from the other girl. Lovinia shook her head until her blonde braids whipped back and forth around her head and shoulders.

"That's fine," Faith said, and then to the older girl, "Your name, please?"

The girl sat up straight and said, "I am Prudence Evans. My father is the telegraph operator. My sister is six years old. I am nine years old. My brother is thirteen—" The oldest pupil, a boy, had jerked one of Prudence's braids. She swung around and slapped him. "Charley, leave me be. That hurts!"

The big-boned young man rubbed his cheek. "You didn't have to do that in front of the schoolmarm, sis."

"Leave my hair alone."

"Children!" Faith indicated a boy on the end of the front row. "And you are...?"

"Joey. Joey Perkins. My pop is the grocer. I'm seven." Joey had a bit of a lisp. He turned and pointed to a chubby boy a row back. "That's my brother Curtis. He's ten."

Curtis scowled at Joey. "I can say that for myself."

"Thank you, Joey. Curtis, have you anything to add?"

"Yes, miss. I do sums the best."

Faith smiled. "Then you must help me with the younger pupils. Next?"

The other children each took a turn. Charley, Hortense, Mary, Thomas, Paul, Christine, and Martha. Faith tried to keep their names in her head until she had a chance to write them down.

"Now that I know who you are, I will tell you a little about myself," Faith said. "I come from New York City, far away in the east. New York is located principally on an island between the East River and the Hudson River. Can anyone tell me the name of the island where I lived?"

Several pupils raised their hands. Martha knew the correct answer. After giving a lesson on geography and wishing she had a better map, Faith moved on to arithmetic. She allowed Curtis to tutor the four youngest pupils while she taught the older ones a lesson she hoped he could catch up with later. Recess followed. Faith caught her breath, made note of the pupils' names in a seating chart, ate her lunch, and straightened the room a bit. Then she rang the bell to call the children back into the schoolroom.

The rest of the day went swiftly, and when four o'clock came, it took her by surprise. She released the pupils. They went to the back of the room where they found their belongings and left, running as soon as they hit the ground.

The next day was much the same as the first, although Faith also made assignments for cleaning the blackboards and carrying in stove wood.

"You've done well today, children," she said as four o'clock approached. "Thomas, it's your turn to clean the blackboards. The rest of you may go, but remember to clean your slates tonight."

The pupils hurried out of the room, laughing and chatting with their friends. Thomas asked if Miss Bannister wanted him to lay a fire for the next day.

"I don't think we'll need it yet, Thomas. The weather is still quite warm. Perhaps tomorrow?"

As Thomas started his task at the blackboard, a masculine voice spoke from the doorway. "The weather can turn bad in fifteen minutes, miss."

Faith turned to see a handsome man standing at the back of the classroom. He removed his hat and held it in one hand while, with the other, he smoothed his black hair carefully to each side of his head from a center parting.

"Rance Hunter at your service, miss." He made a slight bow. "You'd best have wood laid up in case of a storm," he added, his black eyes snapping with deviltry.

Faith admired the man's thick, full-bodied hair. Then her eyes returned to his face, and she noted that his Roman nose was perfectly symmetrical beneath black brows. She began to smooth wrinkles from the front of her skirt.

"I'll put a few sticks in the stove for you, if you'd like," Mr. Hunter said.

She nodded. Realizing how easily the man had entered the schoolroom without her hearing him, she glanced at Thomas. He had nearly finished with his job, as he was cleaning the erasers. She got his attention with a hand on his shoulder. "Thank you, Thomas. You've helped a great deal."

The boy put the erasers in their places, looked

up at her, and then at the man. "Is it okay if I leave now, if you don't need anything else?"

She meant to say, "Please stay here with me." She couldn't think of another task to set for him, however, so she replied, "That will be fine. Thank you."

As the boy left, Mr. Hunter backed away from the stove, brushing his hands together after laying the fire. "That bundle of sticks should be easy to light if a storm blows up."

His gaze went on too long and became a stare; she repressed the desire to squirm.

At length, he asked, "Have you made plans for supper? It'd please me to take you to the restaurant and buy your meal."

Faith's eyes went a bit wide. *He has a high opinion of himself.* After recovering from her surprise, she said, "I must decline your kind offer, Mr. Hunter. I have several matters to attend to this evening."

The man frowned, said, "Have it your way," and left the schoolhouse.

Faith watched his departure, slowly relaxing. *I suppose I haven't seen the last of Mr. Rance Hunter.*

~*~*~

To Slim's consternation, the cottonwood lay across the corral fence all week long, and Mr.

Ramsey hemmed and hawed every day about it, still seeing visions in the branches. More than once, Slim had to send a cowhand to round up escaped horses.

On Saturday morning, the boss's head seemed to have cleared enough to give Slim orders. "McHenry, today is a half-work day because of the social. Get that fool cottonwood cut up and stack the wood in the back lot where it won't burn anything down when we light it up."

"That'll make a fine bonfire, boss."

Slim couldn't get anybody to do the job. Every cowhand had a reason why he couldn't use the old two-man saw on the tree. Seeing the excuses stacked against him, he shrugged and assigned himself and Curly to the job.

Curly wasn't much pleased with the hot, sweaty chore, but he dug in after a little persuasion from Slim's cash hoard.

The day was hot for September. By midmorning, both Curly and Slim were puffing and blowing with the heat of the exercise and the slowness of the chore.

At this rate I won't get to the dance social before the last dance set's over, Slim thought. Another trickle of sweat ran down past his ear. *It must be eighty degrees in the shade.*

Curly frowned at him. "Slim, you pulling on your side, or am I doing all the doggone work over here?"

"I was thinking the same thing about you." Slim watched Baldy Babbitt go by carrying a pair of buckets containing water. *Dang that lazy Babbitt! He's headed for the bunkhouse to slick up for the party.* Slim pushed harder on the saw and hoped the man would stumble over the black dog lying in the shade by the door and spill his water. No such luck. He stepped over the dog and through the door. *Maybe on his way out...*

Disgusted with the man, Slim jerked on the handle.

Curly grunted with exertion. "This old saw must be duller than a butter knife," he wheezed.

Slim checked the time by the sun. "You thinking what I'm thinking?" He put more muscle into the effort.

"We ain't gonna get this done before quittin' time?" Curly did more work on the next pass.

"Yup."

They sped up, and the stringy trunk finally separated. Both of them took a quick breather, then started on the next cut.

At least the horses get to rest for a while, Slim thought. The team was tied to the fence in the shade until he and Curly cut more sections of wood to haul away. One horse moved in the traces, switching his tail to keep off flies. The other nickered and shook his head.

About 11 o'clock, they commenced dragging

wood again, one or two sections of trunk at a time, whatever the chain would fit around. When they'd hauled all of the sections they'd cut, Curly sat down, taking another breather and letting the horses do the same, while Slim freed up the logs. He unwrapped the last turn and tossed the chain behind the team.

Morning and the best part of the afternoon evaporated before they finished, and when they'd put up the team and were busy washing themselves, it was so late that Curly said he maybe was too exhausted to go into town.

Slim shook his head in disbelief, water droplets flying off his hair. "Aw, you won't miss that dance social for nothing. You always have too much fun at them."

"What's the use of going to a dance if I can't move my aching body enough to do the hoedown?" Curly whined.

"You're just bellyaching. Stay here if you've the notion. Nothing's keeping me home tonight."

In the end, Curly found enough strength to fork his horse and accompany Slim after all.

~*~*~

That's too tight, Faith thought, and re-tied the sash of her dress. It wouldn't do for the school teacher to faint at her first outing.

She fluffed out the bow and looked back

toward the looking glass hanging on the wall of her bedroom, wondering if she fit the picture of— what had Charley called it?—a schoolmarm.

I know I can do the job well enough, she thought, smoothing the front of her dress. She checked the slight tilt of her hat and pinched her cheeks, just a little. A faint, rosy glow responded, and she breathed a sigh of relief.

"A perfect schoolmarm," she said, and nodded. She turned to the door, picking up her drawstring reticule. Then she cast another glance in the direction of the glass. "Bitter Springs, here I come," she whispered, and blew out the lamp.

Slim and Curly arrived late to the dance and spent most of the first fifteen minutes leaning against the wall, watching the girls as they danced by in their best clothes.

Slim saw one gal he'd almost decided to court, Edith Longstreth. The man dancing with her now had laid a claim on her before Slim got up the nerve to ride to her poppa's house and ask if he could come a-calling. That was too bad, 'cause she was the best-looking of all the girls around. A doleful regret settled on him for letting her get away, and he vowed that wouldn't happen to him again.

He was just peeling himself off the wall,

aiming to see what the town ladies had provided for refreshments, when Ralph Perkins banged on a pie tin to get everyone's attention and said he had an announcement. He beckoned for someone to come forward out of the crowd, smiled expansively and said, "This little lady coming up here now is our new school teacher, Miss Faith Bannister. She comes to us from New York City and has a wonderful knowledge of the arts and sciences, as well as mathematics and grammar. Let's make her feel welcome."

Mr. Perkins proceeded to clap, and several other people around him joined in. A few of the ruder members of the audience whooped and whistled. By this time, the lady in question had made her way through the throng and turned to face in Slim's direction. His jaw went slack.

Miss Faith Bannister was quite a sight for a country boy to take in. She wore a white dress with those large, puffed, leg-o-mutton sleeves. She sported a light-blue ribbon tied around her little waist and had a sort of hat on her head. It wasn't big enough to hide the fact that her hair was the color of goldenrod in a meadow. A little bag hung from her wrist by a pair of strings. Slim stared, shifted his feet, and forgot Edith Longstreth. The only woman on earth stood before him across the room.

Curly came up behind Slim and gave him a

nudge with his shoulder. "Close your mouth. You're droolin' all over the floor."

Slim obeyed and swallowed hard. He couldn't be drooling, 'cause his mouth was dry as sand. He couldn't even raise enough spit to bicker with Curly. He only shook his head and adjusted his hat low over his eyes.

A voice called from the crowd. "How much 'perience does she have?"

A flush crept over the lady's face. Slim bristled, wanting to offer a challenge to the man who had besmirched her reputation by asking such a question, but he couldn't tell who had spoken. He heard grumbling in front of him. Others had the same question in mind.

"Miss Bannister is well educated," Mr. Perkins avowed, somewhat heatedly. "You won't be disappointed in my selection."

"I will do my best for your children," Miss Bannister said in a clear, soft voice. She moved through the crowd, coming in his direction as she greeted folks. In a moment, a milky-white hand extended into his eyesight. "I'm Faith Bannister," said the soft voice. "Have you children enrolled in the school?"

Slim raised his head and looked into misty-blue eyes surrounded by a fair face on which the flush had not totally abated. He pulled off his hat and shifted it from hand to hand before deciding which mitt to put forward to meet hers. "Howdy, miss. No, miss. I'm Slim McHenry of the Four Rivers Ranch. Pleased to meet you." After giving her hand one pump, he let it go.

"It's a pleasure indeed, Mr. McHenry." Her voice was so soft that he strained to hear it over the hubbub.

"Ah, I'm—I'm just Slim, miss."

Miss Bannister raised one hand to cover her mouth. He could tell she was smiling. *Did I make a joke?*

"Why, yes, that's quite correct." She lowered her fingers to chin level. Sure enough, she was smiling at him. "I've no doubt you're very nice, also."

Slim's face burned as though he squatted next to a branding fire. He gulped, said something nonsensical, and hoped Miss Bannister would walk on by.

Instead, Curly elbowed him in the ribs and chuckled. "You'll have to cut him some slack, miss," he said to the lady. "He's working with only half a brain. Our boss made him foreman a couple weeks ago, and he's still finding his way." Curly winked at the schoolmarm. "Now take me, miss. My name is Curly Price. I have all my brains in place, and I'm the best rider and cowhand in the whole valley."

Slim glared at Curly. Bragging like that was

underhanded and self-serving, and besides, he was dead wrong. *Slim* was the best cowhand in three counties, and Curly darn well knew it. Slim had to get the lady away from that rascal.

Just then, the musicians played a chord.

"Would you care to dance, Miss Bannister?" Slim crammed his hat on his head and held out his hand.

"Why yes. That would be lovely," she replied, putting her smooth little hand into his rough one. "I would be honored."

Slim did his best to bow gracefully over her hand, then led her onto the sawdust-covered floor.

What a wonder that dance was. Slim swore that a higher power led his legs around the room, for he hardly stumbled at all. Miss Bannister smiled and waltzed and seemed happy to follow his lead.

At one point, she gazed into his eyes and asked, "Did I understand your friend correctly? You're the foreman of the Four Rivers Ranch?"

"I am." He missed a step and almost trod on her toes. "I'm still learning the job." How long would the dance last? He was torn between running off in shame at his stumble and holding the lady in his arms forever.

"Perhaps someday soon you could show me around the ranch, Mr. McHenry."

"That would be my great pleasure, miss." Slim smiled at her, and something warm welled up in his chest. "I can show you around the whole area, if you'd like."

She smiled. "Let's start with your ranch first."

"How about next Saturday? I'll bring a wagon and pick you up about nine in the morning."

"That sounds delightful indeed," she said, looking thoughtful. "Do you mind if I ask Mrs. Perkins to come, as well?"

"Sounds good to me. I'll meet you in front of the general store, then. Nine o'clock."

She smiled again, and then the dance came to an end, and he released her from his arms.

"I will be waiting," she murmured. Then she was gone, and his arms felt empty, robbed of her warmth and grace.

Shortly thereafter, Slim was drinking punch from a little glass cup when he looked up to see Rance Hunter making an entrance. Slim couldn't miss him. Hunter guffawed at something Nick Bray said then made a protest that there was no liquor bar set up. He weaved a bit as he walked.

I reckon he's already had a snoot full of strong drink.

The problem was, Hunter walked right up to Miss Bannister. He asked her to dance, but she looked reluctant. Then he loudly bragged on his close kinship to Amos Ramsey, owner of the largest ranch in the valley. The schoolmarm finally agreed to dance with him.

Hunter spun his way around the room with the lady in his embrace. She was trying to make conversation, and he smiled down at her with a smooth look that made Slim's stomach queasy. He didn't know what it was about Amos Ramsey's stepson that set his teeth on edge, but the fact was, Slim detested the man.

Slim disposed of his cup so that as soon as the musicians stopped playing, he was on hand to rescue Miss Bannister. "Would you like refreshments, miss?" he asked, taking her by the elbow.

"Yes," she said, looking a bit confused, for Hunter still held tightly to her other hand. "That would be lovely." She turned to Hunter. "Thank you for the dance, Mr. Hunter. I'm sure it was delightful." She got her hand free and turned her attention to Slim. "Where is the refreshment table, Mr. McHenry?"

"In the schoolyard, miss." He put pressure on her elbow to steer her away from Hunter, who looked at Slim as though he wished him dead. Slim hustled the girl toward the door.

They stepped outside, and Miss Bannister looked at Slim's fingers gripping her elbow. He let go, feeling abashed that he'd been clutching at her so tight.

"I like this better," she said, slipping her hand around the crook of his elbow. His mood changed some as they strolled into the glare of the torches set around the yard. With her on his arm, he felt ten feet tall. She pointed out what she fancied among the array of tasty tidbits the ladies of the town had provided, and Slim juggled two plates and served up the food.

They sat on a bench built for the youngsters under a stand of cottonwoods alongside the schoolyard fence. Slim made certain Miss Bannister was settled before he went back to the line for liquid refreshment.

He returned carrying two cups of fruit punch. Miss Bannister was picking at the food on her plate. He presented her the cup with a slight bow.

She smiled and took a sip. "That's very tasty. Thank you. I was becoming a bit parched."

Slim thought he grew another foot taller.

He sat beside her. Miss Bannister asked about the work he did as foreman. Her interest made him feel special. Soon he forgot his sweaty hands and gawky feet and talked his fool head off. He scarcely touched his food, and when the musicians signaled the commencement of the second half of the dance, he had nearly an entire plate load of food remaining.

When Miss Bannister said she didn't have a

partner for the next dance, and asked if he would kindly oblige her by whirling her around the floor—or words of the same meaning—he gladly abandoned the plate. Once they'd entered the building, Slim took her in his arms for the dance, and believe it or else, he floated her around that floor like he'd been born to the ballroom.

I feel like a gentleman. Me, a rude cowman, ill-schooled and all rough around the edges, he thought. *I swear it's her doing, smiling upon me like that.*

Slim felt a turning inside his chest and realized that he'd just fallen in love with Miss Faith Bannister.

Chapter 3

❝ It is *not* my turn," Baldy Babbitt insisted, punctuating his point with a finger jabbed into Slim's chest.

"Hold your horses," Slim rejoined. "Which of you fellows mended fence last week?" He looked around at a circle of antagonistic faces staring at him.

Baldy didn't yield his place in front of Slim. "It was me 'n' Banjo. We was the ones who done the work. It ain't right you want us to dig post holes this week too."

Slim searched his love-befuddled memory. After a moment he said, "You're right, Baldy. I was wrong. Get back to the herd. Banjo, you're off the hook too." He gestured with his head.

"See now," Baldy said. "You should've said that right off when I brung the sitchiation to your notice. You're larning, McHenry." He caught Banjo's eye, and they moved away.

As the two men left the circle, Slim swung his gaze over the other cowhands. "Hunter, you and Bray are up for the post hole digging. Get a move on."

Hunter mumbled something foul in a low voice, gave Slim a hard look, and marched off. Bray followed, looking over his shoulder at Slim.

Slim endeavored to hide his shudder. *Those two together spelled trouble.* He could feel it to his toes as he assigned out the other work for the day.

A few days later, finding his stock tally short, Slim tapped Curly to accompany him into town for supplies for a pursuit.

"Fifteen head," Slim said, a grim set to his mouth. "This rustling has to stop."

Faith listened as Charley recited a poem she'd taught the class last week. His resigned face sagged in surprise when Mary began to scream.

Her piercing shrieks continued as Faith jumped to her feet and rushed around her desk to offer aid and comfort. By then, Mary had climbed atop her desk, hauling Hortense along with her. Her cries turned to sobs, and she clung to Hortense with all her might.

Faith stopped short and slowly motioned Charley back toward the corner. A rattlesnake slithered under a desk then veered into the aisle near the stove and began to contort itself into a coil. "Children, get up on your desks," she managed to say through a constricted throat.

Puzzled but obedient, they scrambled up then looked around the floor for danger. The older girls cried out in alarm.

"Charley, there's a pistol in my desk drawer. Please bring it to me," Faith said.

He found it, making snuffling noises.

Faith put her hand backward to receive the gun, as she dared not take her eyes off the reptile. She adjusted her grip as she said in a low voice, "Paul, please tell the class what manner of snake that is."

"Wa-wa-western duh-duh-diamondbuh-back rah-rah-rattlesnake, miss," Paul stuttered while Faith took a step forward. The girls all sucked in their breath in unison.

"No, miss!" wailed Mary's sister, Christine.

Faith took another step, fighting her panic. She had to be close enough for her shots to count. She hoped Father would be vindicated in his decision to educate and train his daughter as well as if she'd been a son.

From the corner, Charley sniffed. Faith placed her left hand on Joey's desktop and leaned forward as the snake began to shake its rattle.

God, please guide my aim, she prayed and grasped the gun with both hands. She extended her arms, slowed her breathing, and sighted on the head. Then she held her breath and squeezed the trigger once, then twice more for good measure.

Bang! Bang! Bang!

She dimly heard an uproar over the ringing in her ears; remembered the children. She let out her breath, took another, and said, "Go! Out the door."

Feet clumped on the floorboards as the children escaped. Faith heard her heart thumping in the dense silence that followed. Then heavier footfalls pounded into the schoolhouse and she looked up. Slim McHenry hesitated two steps inside the door, staring at the headless snake. He rushed down the aisle.

Faith began to shake.

Slim kicked the dead snake aside, took the pistol from Faith's hand, and laid it on a desk. Then he grasped both her hands in his and asked, "You killed it?"

She couldn't stop shaking, but nodded.

"Holy Hannah," Slim murmured.

She wished he would embrace her like Father would have done. She looked into his eyes, saw something approaching awe. His gaze softened, he enveloped her in strong arms, and she gave in to sobs, just as Mary had done.

"There, there, miss," he whispered. "What a grand woman you are."

~*~*~

As he left the schoolhouse, Slim thought how lucky he and Miss Faith had been that she was able to compose herself before anyone else had arrived to investigate the gunfire. Just after she'd left his arms, quite a crowd had gathered to comment on the lady's bravery and to examine the snake.

He mentally shook himself, picked up Curly and the supplies, and got on the trail of another kind of snake, a human who stole cattle.

They didn't know much. Was the rustler armed? Would the chase take them into Pleasant Valley, where the feud was winding down but a stranger was still a stranger? Intruding into his assessment of the dangers he and Curly might face was the hum in his nerve endings lingering from his embrace with Miss Faith. He'd only offered her needed comfort, but Great Nellie! It had felt mighty good to hold her for a moment, to indulge in a dream.

Unfortunately, they lost the tracks of the cattle on an area covered with splintered malapai rock. Although they cast around for any sign of the herd, they came up unsuccessful.

"Who drives cows into this loose stuff?" Curly complained.

Slim pressed his lips together tightly before he

spoke. "Some varmint who knows we're coming after him." There was nothing to do but return to the ranch empty-handed.

After breakfast the next morning, Slim asked the cook, "Has anybody been missing meals the last few days?"

"Only you and Mr. Price," Mrs. Marks said. She thought for a moment. "Mr. Hunter did ask me to pack extra victuals for him and Mr. Bray while they worked on the fence line. He said it was a waste of time to come in for meals if they could stay out and finish the job."

That made sense. It didn't sound like Hunter's usual attitude about work, but Slim had emphasized the importance of fixing the rest of the fence. Perhaps the man wanted to get the chore over and done with. He thanked Mrs. Marks and turned away.

Although Slim hadn't caught the cattle thieves, he had work to do before he took Saturday off, when Miss Faith would be visiting the ranch. Warmth flooded his soul at the memory of the embrace he had shared with her. Pleasant as the occurrence had been, he would not dare mention it to anyone. Miss Faith had been under duress. He wouldn't cause her embarrassment.

Stifling his yearning to further his acquaintance with the school teacher, Slim went to work.

~*~*~

Saturday came. Faith stood on the walk in front of Perkins' store, brushing imaginary specks of lint off her dress, and waiting for Slim McHenry to come with his wagon. Mrs. Perkins came out of the store, waving goodbye to her husband.

"I declare, it's mighty kind of you to invite me to accompany you, Miss Faith. I appreciate the time off."

Faith leaned into the street to look down the road. "I don't see Mr. McHenry. Is he late?"

"He'll be along. Slim's a punctual young man."

Faith tried to gather her wits enough to make small talk. "Have you lived here long, Mrs. Perkins?"

"Call me Edith, dearie. Mr. Perkins and I have been here nigh on to six years, now. It seems like we come just yesterday." She also looked down the street.

Faith brushed her dress again. "What could be delaying him?"

"Don't worry. He's not late. It isn't nine o'clock yet."

"It's not? I thought I arrived late." Faith pulled a tiny watch out of her bag and shook it, then held it to her ear. "It's not running."

Mrs. Perkins laid her hand on Faith's arm.

"You're nervous waiting for that good-looking cowboy to show up and meeting Mr. Ramsey and all. It wouldn't surprise me none if he's taken a shine to you."

"Mr. Ramsey? We haven't met."

"Why no. I mean that lanky foreman, Slim McHenry." Mrs. Perkins leaned her head to one side and winked.

Faith drew herself up in righteous indignation. "Mrs. Perkins, I am the school teacher. I didn't come here to find a man or to carry on with a cowboy. You know that's forbidden in my contract."

"I meant no harm, gal."

Faith nodded. She wanted to say, "Just leave it be," but restrained herself. In truth, the foreman intrigued her with his blend of rough and tender attributes. She recalled the strength in his arms around her. Her skin tingled.

A cloud of dust caught her eye. A wagon drawn by two brown horses approached. Slim soon brought the team to a halt in front of the store.

"Good day, ladies!" he shouted, grinning, and dropped to the ground from the seat. "It's a fine day, and there's a breeze curling the tips of the pines. Come take a ride."

"Indeed," Faith said, lowering her tight shoulders. She felt a smile on her lips.

Slim helped Faith onto the seat, then boosted Mrs. Perkins up. He got on the seat beside Faith and turned the horses to retrace his route. "Have you driven through the country before, Miss Faith?" he asked as they pulled into a stand of tall, whispering pines blown by a soft breeze.

"Not since Mr. Dobbs drove me down from the depot."

"I'll bet you were tired then, after the long trip on the train cars. Sit back and relax yourself. Take in the view."

Faith breathed in the sharply sweet scent of pitch, remembering the pine gum one of the pupils had brought her this week. Now here she was on her way to a real ranch. She clasped her fingers together and tried to concentrate on Mr. McHenry's descriptions of ranch life.

"...during the roundup next spring, then we ship the cattle to Chicago for processing. That's a fancy word for slaughter. I hope that don't offend you, Miss Faith." He slapped the horses' rumps with the lines.

Faith swallowed as Slim's arm brushed hers. "Why, no. It's all so interesting."

Mrs. Perkins said, "Don't you scare off our schoolmarm. We want to keep her."

"I must earn my own way in the world. I hope to stay as long as possible, if my work is agreeable to the school board."

"I'm sure there's no problem there, as Ralph—Mr. Perkins—thinks you're a great asset to the community," Mrs. Perkins patted Faith's hand. "My boys love having you as schoolmarm. All they can talk about is how brave you are, killing that snake and all."

Faith bit her lip without replying. She wished to forget the snake.

"You're not worried about what that drunk said at the dance, are you? He don't know the broad side of a barn from his backside."

Faith colored. "Thank you, Mrs. Perkins. I appreciate your support."

"Not at all, child. You'll teach for a term or two, then retire to marry one of our eligible men. We have a bunch of them, and some of them are looking for a wife." Mrs. Perkins chuckled. "Some of 'em don't know they're looking."

Faith felt her face flush. A sidelong glance told her that Slim's face matched her own.

"Ladies," he said in a strangled voice, "watch for the view ahead. Sets my heart a-bumping every time I see it."

They emerged from the pine forest, and the decided nip in the morning air abated with the warmth of the sun. Slim stopped the wagon. Before them, an immense meadow full of dry grass stretched toward the up-thrusting rock of the Mogollon Rim. Patches of cloud fluffed in the sky. Nestled amidst a stand of cottonwoods, a two-story house gleamed white, surrounded by outbuildings. The perpendicular ridge of the Rim, red and brown and topped with majestic pines, stood guardian. The sight took Faith's breath away.

"It's magnificent!" she cried.

"I'm glad you like it. It's a pride to us all," Slim said, twitching the lines to get the horses started again. "Mr. Ramsey spent a good long stretch of years building it up."

Mrs. Perkins chattered away at Faith's side. "It's lovely, just lovely. Imagine me getting the guided tour. I've never seen the place before."

Slim halted the horses in front of the house and got down from the wagon to assist the ladies. Soon they stood on the porch under the slope of the veranda roof, dusting their dresses.

"I got the cook's permission to show you around the house," Slim said. "Come in and look at the fancy gee-gaws."

As they went inside, Faith looked at the glass fan window above the door. A ceiling of stamped tin arched high above them, and a design of yellow roses and thin, gray stripes marched down the papered walls. Dark patches on the wallpaper showed where pictures had been removed. This was a lone man's house now.

Faith turned and looked around her. A door

stood open to her left, through which she saw a
room decorated with mounted animal heads. She
felt a pang, remembering the security she'd always
felt in her father's study. She turned away and
looked about. An attached staircase led to the upper
floor. Another door led to a room on the right. Along
a passage, she saw a third door, which she guessed
was the kitchen.

"It's very lovely, Mr. McHenry," Faith said. "Is
your employer out on the grounds?"

Slim's mouth twitched. "Ah, he's not feeling well.
Hasn't been for weeks. We finally had to put him to
bed."

"The poor man!" exclaimed Mrs. Perkins. "What
ails him?"

"Not sure, ma'am. His sight is getting bad, but
worse than that, he's, ah, not keeping food down,
and he sees things that ain't there."

"Has the doctor been to see him?" Faith asked.

"Well, no. Ol' Amos refuses any caretaking."

"That's nonsense!" Mrs. Perkins said. "Men can
be so impossible."

Faith laid her hand on Slim's arm. "We should
look in on him."

Mrs. Perkins agreed.

"He won't like it."

"I insist. He may be very ill."

Slim made a face. "I'll take you to him, but I hope
he don't yell at you ladies." He started up the stairs,

and Faith and Mrs. Perkins hurried to keep up.

"McHenry!" a voice roared from above their heads. "Why did you get rid of that angel?"

"Oh, he's having a bad spell," Slim moaned. "He's carryin' on about that angel again."

Faith caught up to him. "What angel is that?"

"For the last little while, he's been talkin' about seeing an angel. A week or two."

"He must have the doctor to see him," Mrs. Perkins puffed as she joined them on the landing.

Slim shook his head. "He won't do it, ma'am." He cringed as foul language poured over the transom from a room ahead. "Begging your pardon, ladies. He's getting mighty rank in his language. Maybe you'd prefer to take that tour of the grounds instead?"

"Definitely not!" Faith exclaimed. "The man's clearly in distress. Mrs. Perkins and I can forgive his language. Isn't that so?"

"Certainly, dearie. He's not in his right mind."

"He don't appear to be," Slim agreed, halting before the door and biting his lip. "Ladies, you can still change your minds..."

"Lead the way, Mr. McHenry," Faith said. "The man needs assistance, not censure."

"Thank you for your Christian attitude, miss," Slim said, and opened the door.

Faith hesitated before stepping into the room, steeling herself for any verbal abuse Mr. Ramsey might hand out. She took a deep breath and crossed the threshold.

Amos Ramsey lay in a huge, four-poster bed with a hat hung on each post. Clad in long underwear, he had clearly been covered with a muslin sheet and a thin quilt, but the bedclothes were now strewn on the floor. He thrashed about with jerky movements, muttering nonsense about angels, and cursing encyclopedically.

Faith gave a cry and ran to the side of the bed. She pressed one hand to his face, which she found hot, dry, and quite red. "Oh my, oh my. Mr. Ramsey, you must have a doctor right away."

Although the man did not answer, he quieted under Faith's touch, grunting incoherently. She blinked to keep back tears. The poor, tormented soul!

"Yes, indeed," Mrs. Perkins chimed in, approaching the bed from the other side. She clicked her tongue as she touched his forehead. "The man is delirious with fever." She turned to Slim. "What has Mr. Ramsey been eating?"

Slim thought a moment. "Nothing more than we all eat, ma'am—beef, beans, and biscuits."

"Hmm." Mrs. Perkins eyed Mr. Ramsey's limbs. "He's not snake-bit, is he?"

"No, ma'am. There's not been any swelling, and two weeks with snake venom would have seen him dead by now."

Faith looked at Slim, her eyes brimming with tears. "You must send someone for the doctor this instant. He may die."

"I don't know, miss—"

"She's right, Mr. McHenry. You don't want Mr. Ramsey's death on your conscience." Mrs. Perkins made as though to shove Slim out the door, and he backed up.

"He does seem mighty low. Worse than before."

"You're the foreman, isn't that right?" Mrs. Perkins shook her finger in Slim's face. "It's up to you to make decisions when your boss isn't well enough to do so, correct?"

"I—I guess so. Yes, I suppose I'd better do that." Slim turned and stepped into the corridor. He returned immediately. "You ladies will stay with him?"

Faith nodded, and Mrs. Perkins murmured, "Of course. Go along, Mr. McHenry."

He did.

"Who's there? Who's there?" Mr. Ramsey began to thrash again. "I can't see. Who is it?"

Faith caught his hand in hers and patted it. "I'm the school teacher, sir, and this lady keeps the store in town. You're ill, but the doctor will be here soon."

"Fool doctor," Mr. Ramsey said, pulling his hand free. "He won't see my angel."

"Where is it, sir?"

Amos turned his face toward Faith's and squinted. "I don't know you, do I? Fool eyes. Don't work proper." He moved his arm spasmodically, pointing toward the top of the wardrobe. "It's sittin' on top, guarding me. You see it?"

Faith looked. "Of course. Such lovely hair."

"I can't see it clear anymore. What happened to my eyes?"

"You must rest. Mrs. Perkins and I will remain with you until the doctor arrives." She turned to her companion. "We must sponge his face and arms to cool his fever, and get him to drink water. I've learned that much about sickroom care from a relative."

"Good idea. I'll fetch a basin of water and cloth. The cook will know where they're to be found." She left the room.

Two hours later, Slim brought the doctor into the room.

"Ladies," the man greeted them, removing his hat along with his coat. "Let's see what we have here." He opened his black bag and produced an implement that he placed into his ears and the other end upon Mr. Ramsey's chest. "Ah. Rapid heartbeat. How long has your ticker been racing, Amos?"

"Fool doctor," Amos said. He followed that

with his view of the man's parentage.

"Let me see your tongue." He wielded a flat stick in Amos's direction and managed to use it briefly. "Hmm." He raised Amos's eyelids one by one. "Hmm," he repeated.

"Fool eyes don't work right," Amos complained.

"Hmm," the doctor said a third time. "You're feverish."

"We've been wiping his face and arms, doctor," Faith said. "He hasn't cooled much."

"Slim, how long has he been in this state?"

"Couple weeks, doc. He talks about angels in trees and such."

"He's sitting over yonder." Amos raised a jerky hand and pointed.

"How bad is he, doc?"

The doctor took Slim to one side, whispering his opinion, but Faith heard enough.

"...nursing care, around the clock, if possible."

Letting all social propriety go, she intruded herself into the conversation. "I know the very person to care for him, Mr. McHenry. My cousin is a trained nurse. She can be here in three or four days, if you will send her a telegram."

"Excellent," the doctor said. "Make the arrangements, McHenry. I can't be held accountable for his decline if he's left alone."

Chapter 4

"**D**earest Clarissa, I'm glad you've arrived safely."

Clarissa hugged her cousin fiercely, and then Faith drew her over to the best chair in the room and had her sit. A cowboy calling himself Baldy Babbitt had fetched Clarissa from the train station, and she was to rest here at Faith's house while Mr. Babbitt filled an order for the ranch at the store.

Clarissa looked around as she removed her hat and gloves. "You have a cozy situation here."

"Thank you, cousin. May I bring you a refreshment?" Faith asked.

"Perhaps a glass of water, if you don't mind," Clarissa said. "It's a relief to sit still. Crossing the country on the train cars was quite an experience."

"You have only another hour of wagon travel to the ranch, then you won't feel all of that disconcerting swift movement." Faith brought Clarissa a sandwich on a plate in addition to the water. "Please eat a bite. You must be famished."

Clarissa smiled. "I suppose I am, dear. If truth

be told, I am anxious for Mr. Ramsey. You say he is having visions?" She bit into the sandwich.

"He is, and he complains of poor sight. Also, his movements are jerky."

After she swallowed, Clarissa said, "My first thought was that he's suffered a brain stroke, but he has use of all his limbs?"

"Yes."

"And the doctor has no diagnosis?"

"He seems mystified. He's ruled out insect or snake bite, but he doesn't have any other ideas to account for Mr. Ramsey's symptoms."

"I suppose I shall be limited to treating those symptoms, then."

"You're an excellent nurse. I'm confident you will be able to restore the man to health."

"God willing," Clarissa said, brushing crumbs off her bodice front.

Faith smiled. "I'm certain Mrs. Marks will appreciate your arrival. She's the cook, but I hear she's been wearing herself to a frazzle tending to the man over the last few days."

As it was Saturday, Faith insisted on accompanying Clarissa the rest of the way to the Four Rivers Ranch to see her settled.

When they arrived, Clarissa said, "I wonder if Mr. Ramsey has had a change of diet. Perhaps he is eating something that disagrees with his constitution."

"Mr. McHenry thought not."

A convivial woman let them in, and inside, they found the house in an uproar.

Identifying herself as Mrs. Marks, the woman said, "The old boy is having conniptions. He wants his whiskey. Now." She winced at the curses coming from the second floor.

"Strong drink can't be good for him," Faith said.

"Doc says he can have one glass after supper," Mrs. Marks retorted. She addressed herself to Clarissa, saying, "Come along. We'll put your things in your room, ma'am, and I'll introduce you to the old geezer."

When the cousins entered the sickroom, Mrs. Marks made the promised introductions.

"Mr. Ramsey, I'm here to nurse you," Clarissa said. "I'll have your health increasing just as soon as Doctor Quincy determines what ails you."

"Fool doctor said I could have whiskey. Where is it?" Amos demanded.

"You must eat your supper first. Mrs. Marks will bring it presently."

"I'm not hungry. Who did you say you are? Come closer."

"Clarissa Pembroke, sir. I'm the trained nurse Doctor sent for."

"Trained nurse?" He peered at her. "You don't look ugly. Not boney. Not like that one." He gestured toward Faith and smirked at Clarissa. "Are you giving me a bath tonight, nurse?"

"I'll clean you up after you eat your supper," Clarissa answered.

Amos smacked his lips. "Bring the food. I want a shave, too."

"We'll see." Clarissa raised her eyebrows and took Faith into a corner. "I can handle this case. He's full of ginger, but I believe he craves attention. Will you take notes of his actions for me?"

"Yes. I'll sit out of your way."

Faith watched as Clarissa assisted Amos with his meal, then washed him up and trimmed his whiskers.

"You have a nice start to an attractive beard," Clarissa said. "You won't require a shave."

"Hey! I figured you'd dunk me in a tub. I'm paying for your nursing skills, aren't I? I want them used right."

"Mr. Ramsey, the doctor and I will determine the best use of my skills. You needed only a minor cleansing and a trim. Now, let's see about your whiskey."

"Aye, my whiskey."

Mrs. Marks brought a nearly empty bottle and a tumbler. "Good thing Mr. Babbitt bought a new bottle today," she said. "This one is on its last legs." She poured the whiskey and started to hand the drink to Clarissa, but stopped and looked into the glass. "That's odd. Something fell out with the whiskey." She put a finger into the glass and pulled out an object. She held it on her palm. "Look at that. What do you make of it, ma'am?"

Faith came over and watched Clarissa examine the gray splinter. "That certainly has no business in the bottle."

Clarissa agreed, picking up the object and working her fingers over it. "Organic, but not smooth. It has broken edges. It's not a tree or plant limb. Is it part of a seed?"

"It may be, although it's a bit large for a seed," Faith said.

"Indeed. How did it get into the bottle?" Clarissa asked.

Mrs. Marks shrugged. "I can't say, ma'am."

Clarissa took the tumbler and poured the liquid into the chamber pot, over Amos's objection. "Where was the bottle kept? Locked up, I trust?" she asked the cook.

"In the common room, in a cabinet. I don't think there's a key anymore."

"Hmm," Clarissa said.

"I want my whiskey!" Amos roared.

"There will be a slight delay," she said to Amos, then turned to Mrs. Marks. "I won't give him anything from that bottle. Please show me where it was kept."

"Surely. I thought it would be used up, so I put the new bottle in its place."

"I'll keep watch," Faith said, motioning toward Mr. Ramsey.

~*~*~

Rance slipped into the house from the back door after finding the cook missing. *Lucky me,* he thought, looking into the room where Amos kept his whiskey supply. *Nobody's here.* He crossed to a cabinet, pulled it open, and took down the bottle.

"New?" he whispered, then swore. He'd have to take care pulling the cork or someone would see that the bottle had been opened. He set to work, and when the stopper was free, he took a square of brown paper from his pocket and opened it.

He was in the act of pouring powdered seed into the bottle when he heard two women's voices coming from the staircase. He swore again, then quickly crumpled the paper and thrust the cork into the bottle. He hit it with the heel of his hand to seat it, put the bottle back on the shelf, and hustled through the door to the kitchen, where he held his breath, not daring to go out the back door yet.

"I feed him the same as before he went strange," the cook was saying. "It's not my food."

"Has he taken a fall that would result in an injury to the head?" the second woman asked. Her voice was unknown to him. Who was this in the house?

Before the cook answered, the stranger asked another question. "Did you leave the door to the cabinet ajar when you brought up the whiskey?"

"I did not." The cook sounded put upon. "I always close them doors."

"Hmm," said the stranger. "Mr. Ramsey will be obliged to forego his liquor tonight. I can't allow him to drink from a suspect bottle."

"Right you are," the cook agreed. "Whoever goes into town next can bring another."

Rance mentally cursed the women, whose sudden descent had caused his careless error. He tiptoed across the kitchen and eased open the back door. With a little luck, he would be the chosen errand boy. He'd have to get a new supply of seeds and smash them up tomorrow.

When Slim saw Hunter and Bray at supper, he felt relieved. The perimeter fence finally had been repaired; the ranch wouldn't lose cows in that direction.

In the morning, though, he didn't feel as confident, so he asked Curly to ride out with him to inspect the work.

Coming upon abandoned rolls of barbed wire

and loose strands hanging on the fence posts, Slim swore under his breath. Had Hunter and Bray even come out here? He surveyed the area but found no recent camp spot. "Them buzzards! Where have they been?"

Curly spat on the ground between his horse and Slim's. "When did you send them here?"

Slim calmed himself enough to consider. "Day before the cattle tally came up short."

Curly took out cigarette makings and looked at Slim.

Slim looked at Curly. He closed his eyes, realization heavy on his lids. "Hunter asked the cook to pack food for them so they could fix the fence," Slim growled. "They never did the work. He's stealing cattle from his own old man."

The clock hands crept slowly from three thirty toward four o'clock, and Faith almost regretted her choice to become a school teacher. Some of the children had been unruly today, and she could hardly wait to dismiss them so she could retreat to her house and close out the world.

A sound at the rear of the room drew her attention. *Joey, if you're playing tricks again*—But then she raised her eyes to see Rance Hunter at the back of the room, holding onto the doorjamb with a hand clad in a leather riding glove.

"We're gonna have supper together tonight," he said, slurring his words.

Faith caught her breath. Petticoats rustled as girls turned sideways to see who had come in.

"Get rid uh these kids," he demanded, taking a few unsteady steps into the room.

She drew herself up and started toward him. "School keeps until four o'clock, Mr. Hunter."

"Not today, it don't."

"You're setting these children a poor example!"

"Brats'll grow up anyway," he said, leering at her. He lurched closer and put forward both gloved hands to grasp Faith's face.

"Miss!" Charley said, alarmed.

She winced at the unpleasant mix of the odors of liquor and leather coming from Mr. Hunter's person, and she put out a stiff arm to repel his advance. His chest came to rest against her palm, and he stopped. She pushed him back down the aisle. "You will leave the premises, Mr. Hunter."

The man resisted the pressure on his chest, but he stumbled backward as she pushed harder. He crouched a bit, and his eyes drilled into hers with a withering look. "You'll regret treating me like this," he said. "I'll be the big man hereabouts soon enough."

At the venom in his voice, Faith took half a step backward. What did he mean by his claim?

A glance at the look of terror on Lovinia's face made Faith remember her charges.

"You *will* leave," she repeated, resolving to protect the children. She stiffened her voice into brittle shards. "Get out."

He turned and he left, and Faith slammed the door and put her back to it as she tried to slow her breathing to normal.

"Are you all right, miss?" Charley asked, standing in the aisle, brandishing a piece of firewood.

Faith squared her shoulders. "He is gone, children. Let's finish the lesson." She marched on wobbly legs to the front of the classroom and faced the pupils. "Now, whose turn is it?"

~*~*~

As soon as the children left school, Faith hurried to the livery stable and rented a horse. She had just enough time to ride to the ranch before nightfall. She needed to speak with Clarissa.

Faith dismounted at the ranch house, opened the door without knocking, shouted, "Clarissa!" and, at her cousin's answering call, dashed into the kitchen.

"He said he'd be the 'big man' soon enough," Faith said as she finished her account. "He terrified the children."

Clarissa folded her arms and looked pensive. "I'm beginning to suspect that Mr. Ramsey is being poisoned. That fits with the foreign object in his liquor, and Mr. Hunter's brag."

Faith shook her head in disbelief. "A killer in my schoolroom."

Clarissa motioned Mrs. Marks to join them. "Does Mr. Hunter bear his stepfather a grudge?" she asked the cook.

"Oh yes, ma'am," Mrs. Marks said. "His ma spoiled him terrible. He took her death mighty hard and blames Amos Ramsey for it."

"Enough to want him dead?" Faith asked.

The cook shivered. "Ever looked into them bottomless eyes? I'd say he does." She dipped into her apron pocket. "When I swept up earlier, I found this in the common room under the liquor cabinet."

Clarissa took the crumpled paper and straightened it out over the tabletop. She nudged at something. "There's a residue." A brown splinter fell onto the table. She rubbed her finger over the white material on the paper and sniffed it.

"Careful!" Faith said.

"Granular. Not commercial talcum. Not flour, nor powdered sugar. It's coarse, as though someone used a rock to grind an object down." Clarissa wet another finger with her tongue.

"No," Faith cautioned. "Don't taste it."

"I don't suppose a tiny bit will hurt me."

"It might do," Mrs. Marks said, leaning over to inspect the bit on the table. "That pointed piece there could be part of the spine from a seed husk." She straightened. "Jimson weed. That'll drive man or beast mad and kill 'em in the end."

"According to our eminent lecturer, Dr. Harley, such a powder, introduced slowly, would make an effective poison," Clarissa agreed. "I must tell the authorities."

"You must tell *Slim*—I mean, Mr. McHenry." Faith felt her mouth go dry. When had she begun to think of him as *Slim*?

Clarissa said, "I will. Now you must get back to town, dear. I suggest you ask for an escort."

~*~*~

Rance pulled Bray out of the bunkhouse, proposing a smoke before bed.

"Those blamed, wretched women," he said, watching as Bray built his cigarette. "They're on to us."

"Us?"

"They figured out about the poison. We have to get out of here."

Bray lit up. "I haven't drawn any pay yet. Are you going to make up the loss?"

Rance swore. "I'm out of cash. We have to

gather up all the cattle we can grab and high tail it for New Mexico."

Bray lifted an eyebrow as smoke curled from his cigarette.

Rance continued. "We'll put a rope through the mossy-back steer's nose ring. The whole herd will follow."

Bray shrugged. "It could work."

Rance rubbed his fingers together. "Ten o'clock tonight, then. Banjo's snoring won't cover bumping around in the dark, so be as quiet as you can. We can't chance getting caught."

Chapter 5

The next morning, Clarissa introduced a new regimen for Mr. Ramsey: He was to drink a gray liquid she'd concocted from powdered charcoal and milk, and he was to drink it every two hours until she said he'd had enough.

"I'll be gol-darned if I'm gonna take that stuff," he said, snorting in disgust.

"You will drink it down, sir, or I will not be responsible for your care. I believe you have been poisoned, and this remedy will cure that. If you have not been poisoned, it will not harm you. Either way, you *will* drink it."

"The lady means it, boss," Slim said, standing ready to enforce her edict.

Amos grumbled and cursed, but he took the draught, almost gagging at first, then finishing with a shudder. "Poisoned, huh? Who would poison me?" He thought about it for a while, then started to get out of bed, his face dark with anger. "Blast his hide! I knew that weasel was up to no good."

"See? You're better already, sir," Clarissa

pointed out, keeping him from rising. "Not from the remedy, but because you haven't been taking the poison."

"Then I don't need your foul concoction."

"Yes, you do. The poison is still in your system, and must be flushed out. We suspect it was in your whiskey."

"He poisoned my drink?"

Amos tried to hoist himself up, but Slim gently pushed him back. "I'll see to him."

"Go to it, son."

~*~*~

Slim jogged toward the barn until he spotted Curly riding in at a gallop. He waited for him, itching to get his hands around Rance Hunter's throat.

"They're gone," Curly huffed. "The whole herd."

"What?"

"Baldy figures Hunter and Bray took them sometime last night."

Curly dismounted and began to walk his mount in the yard to cool it down.

Slim turned away, then yelled at Curly over his shoulder. "Get another horse saddled and grab a shotgun. Get all the shells you can find."

Slim saddled a horse in record time and added weapons to his own gear.

Curly did as he was told. Slim went to the kitchen for any leftover food Mrs. Marks could put together. He came back with several parcels, which he put in his saddlebags.

As Curly mounted, he said, "The whole outfit wants to go after them."

"No. Just you and me." Slim swung into his saddle. "We'll travel faster and make less noise. You lead out."

Curly shrugged and clicked his tongue to start his horse.

"'By the shores of Gitche Gumee,'" began little Lovinia. "'By the shining Big-Sea-Water,'" she lisped. Lovinia was the last pupil on the program. Parents shifted on the hard benches.

Faith's stomach hurt. It had ever since Mrs. Perkins scurried up to her before the program started and whispered in her ear that Rance Hunter had stolen Amos Ramsey's herd, and that Slim McHenry had taken out after him.

She inhaled and held her breath. *It can't be true. Mrs. Perkins must stop listening to rumors.* She exhaled.

"'Many things Nokomis taught him,'" Lovinia declaimed, curling her hand into her pinafore pocket.

No, Faith thought. *Keep your hands folded together.*

Lovinia took a deep breath, smoothed her pinafore, then folded her hands in front. "'Of the stars that shine in heaven,'" she continued.

Faith frowned at two boys whispering together at the back of the room. A cold chill enveloped her. *It could be true. Slim would chase Hunter down despite the risk.*

"'Saw the moon rise from the water,'" chanted Lovinia, then hesitated. Her mother made an encouraging sound from her seat on the front row. The girl continued. "'Rippling, rounding from the water.'"

She's nearly finished, Faith thought, her mind wandering despite her best effort to concentrate on Lovinia. *Oh Slim, be careful. Rance is like that rattlesnake, beautiful, but dangerous. Oh, take care.*

Faith blinked as the girl at the front of the room curtseyed and smiled, and seemed relieved that her long ordeal was over. The parents and pupils clapped politely, then louder and harder as Faith stood and went to the front of the schoolroom.

"Well done, Miss Bannister," Mr. Evans called.

"Yes, fine work," Mr. Perkins agreed.

"Thank you." At the praise, Faith felt a blush on her cheeks. "On behalf of the pupils of Bitter Springs School, thank you for coming. I'm pleased to show how diligently they have studied and how much they have learned the last few weeks. Refreshments will be served in the schoolyard."

The parents filed outside, where the mothers took charge of serving the food.

Faith sank onto her desk chair and chewed at a snagged nail. *Don't die, Slim. I'll never forgive you if you die.*

"Psst." Slim motioned to Curly from behind the volcanic outcrop. The trail of the herd had skirted the Mormon communities and led through Indian land, but now the terrain had become so rough that he didn't know how Hunter and Bray could possibly push the cows through. The time had come to put a stop to the rustlers before they lost more of Amos's cattle.

"We'll pinch them off here," Slim whispered. "They can't get around that chute without slowing considerable."

"What's your plan?"

"I'll be over behind that black knob and call on them to stop. You cover me."

"Slim—"

"It's got to work. Two beeves went down this morning."

"Shotgun?"

"If you have to. It'll make a mess. Don't put me in your field of fire."

Curly scoffed. "Don't plan to. I don't want your job."

Slim made his way down the back side of the outcrop, then crawled up the malapai knob until he had a view of the oncoming herd.

He didn't have to wait for long. Soon the herd appeared, cloaked in dust.

Bray led the way, his rope tied to a ring in the nose of the old steer. The cattle followed, lowing their displeasure at the hurried pace. Slim let himself slip down the knob and stepped out into the trail.

"Stop there, Bray," Slim called, amazed that his voice didn't shake, because his knees sure did.

"What the—" The man went for his pistol and drew faster than Slim would have thought possible.

Slim threw himself to the side. He winced at pain as he hit the ground, but his own pistol was ready in his hand, and he fired back in the man's direction.

Bray was off his horse, pulling it down for cover. Slim tried to push himself behind the knob, but one of his legs didn't want to work. He glanced down, then back at Bray. "Curly!"

In answer, Curly fired a slug toward Bray, but it went over his head.

Good— not the shotgun. *Keep him pinned down, Curly.* Slim pulled himself behind the knob by hooking his arm around a tree trunk, but he couldn't locate Hunter.

I should have done that first, he chided himself. *I'm not good at this manhunt playacting.*

With several shots aimed at Slim, Hunter revealed his position, but Curly had the shotgun up and swinging. He let it off, and Hunter screamed.

"Give it up, Bray," Slim called.

"Hunter?" Bray shouted.

Hunter didn't answer.

"Blast it," Bray said. "There goes my pay." He threw his pistol over the horse's neck and got to his feet, hands in the air.

Slim looked at his leg. *I need to get that bullet fetched out.* The light faded.

Next thing he knew, Curly shook his shoulder, not gentle at all. "Slim!"

He looked up. Curly's head blocked the sun, which caused a halo around it. "What?"

"I stopped the bleeding, but couldn't get to the bullet. Come on. Stand up. We'll go to Show Low. They have a doc."

He did as he was told, glad to pass the reins of this ornery cayuse over to Curly. Bray sat against a pine, trussed up like a Christmas goose. "He looks secure. Where's Hunter?"

Curly tilted his head to indicate a sack tied across a horse. Slim squinted. Not a sack. Hunter.

"He dead?"

Curly snarled, "Yeah. I've got to tote his dad-blamed carcass back to the ranch."

Slim considered Curly's words. Yep. They would need to haul him back; this rocky malapai didn't make a good burial ground. "How we gonna do this?"

Curly looked off into the trees.

"Well?"

"I told the outfit to follow us."

"You what?"

"You heard me. I said to hold back some." He waved his arm. "Come out, boys. He'll get over being mad soon as we get him to the doc."

~*~*~

Charley had brought Faith a telegram after school. When he'd departed, she'd read it once, then clutched it to her breast. Now her badly shaking hands almost prevented her from reading it again. Almost.

MISS FAITH BANNISTER STOP AM CRIPPLED UP FOR A WHILE STOP HOPE YOU WILL VISIT WHEN I RETURN ON TUESDAY NEXT STOP JEFFERSON DAVIS MCHENRY END

He'd spent money to send her a telegram. He

hadn't mentioned the extent of his injuries, but he had thought of her in his extremity. She crushed the telegram, hearing the paper crackle. *Thank God he's alive.*

On Monday afternoon, Faith announced a school recess for the next day.

"What's the holiday, miss?" Joey asked.

"I must visit a sick friend."

Joey raised his eyebrows at Curtis. "I told you," he said. "Ma was right."

Faith stifled a groan. *That woman!* She had a good heart, though. "Class dismissed."

She waited a moment to pick up her valise before following the pupils out the door. A horse awaited her at the livery. Tomorrow, Slim would return, and she would be at the ranch to greet him. She didn't know what would happen after that.

By the time Curly drove a wagon into the ranch yard the next day, Faith had chewed all of her nails to the quick. She was sure Clarissa could hear her heart thumping as they watched the vehicle approach. How badly was Slim wounded? No one could tell her. Clarissa patted her shoulder. The wagon turned. Slim sat in the back, supported by several blankets. A pretty young woman sat beside him.

Faith gasped, but before she could turn away in dismay, Slim's voice croaked, "Miss Faith," and she had to meet his gaze.

He beckoned to her. Clarissa gave her a push. Faith's legs dragged like wooden fence posts toward the wagon. She stopped and clutched the wagon's sideboard.

Slim gazed up at her and pried one of her hands loose to hold it. He laid his other hand over his heart, like one of her pupils about to recite a poem about everlasting love. His fingers pressed hers insistently. She held her breath. Had her heart stopped? She couldn't hear it in the stillness.

"Miss Faith," Slim said, a little tremor in his voice. "Meet my cousin Betsy from Show Low. She's come along to nurse me back to health." He looked at the cousin and said, "Hoist me up more, Bets," then returned his attention to Faith. "When I'm healed, I'd be honored if you'd allow me to call."

"I'd like that," she whispered as her heart began to thump again, wildly, joyfully.

The next thing she knew, Slim's lips pressed against her cheek, and gladness suffused her entire soul.

"It'll be soon," Slim said. "That's a promise."

The End

ABOUT THE AUTHOR

Marsha Ward writes authentic historical fiction set in 19th Century America, and contemporary romance. She was born in the sleepy little town of Phoenix, Arizona, in a simpler time. With plenty of room to roam among the chickens and citrus trees, Marsha enjoyed playing with neighborhood chums, but always had her imaginary friend, cowboy Johnny Rigger Prescott, at her side. Now she makes her home in a forest in the mountains of Arizona. She loves to hear from her readers.

Connect with her at www.marshaward.com